Twisted Love; Journey

Twisted Love, Volume 1

Mrigendra Bharti

Published by Sellbrochure Vymish Entertainment, 2024.

This is a work of fiction. Similarities to real people, places, or events are entirely coincidental.

TWISTED LOVE; JOURNEY

First edition. June 15, 2024.

Copyright © 2024 Mrigendra Bharti.

ISBN: 979-8227744159

Written by Mrigendra Bharti.

Table of Contents

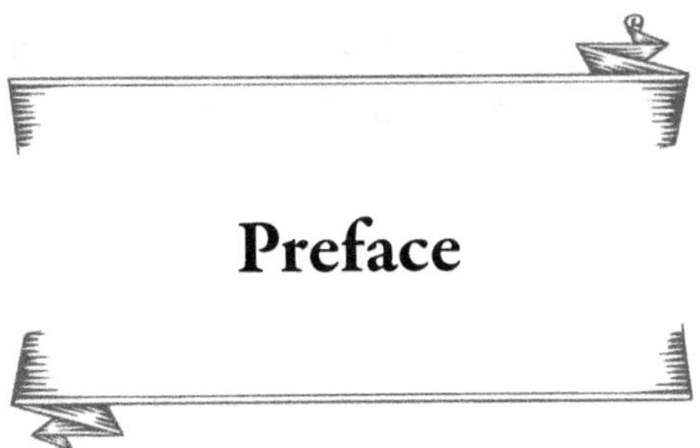

Preface

Love is a complex journey filled with joy, challenges, and unexpected twists. It can uplift and inspire, but it can also test the boundaries of trust and understanding. **Twisted Love** explores the intricacies of relationships through the eyes of a high school girl named Aarushi, whose life takes an unforeseen turn when she discovers a hidden truth about her boyfriend, Rahul.

Aarushi's story is not just about love and heartbreak; it is about self-discovery, acceptance, and the strength to move forward despite life's unexpected complications. As she navigates through the emotional labyrinth of her high school years, she learns invaluable lessons about friendship, loyalty, and the true meaning of love.

This book aims to portray the multifaceted nature of love, emphasizing that it is not confined to a single form or definition. Through the experiences of Aarushi, Rahul, and Sameer, we delve into the beautiful yet intricate patterns that love weaves into our lives.

Twisted Love is a story for anyone who has ever faced the unexpected in their relationships and has emerged stronger and wiser. It is a reminder that while love can be unpredictable, it is also a powerful force that shapes us into who we are meant to be.

Join Aarushi on her journey as she discovers that love, in all its forms, is a path worth exploring, no matter how twisted it may seem.

Prologue

The halls of Greenwood High buzzed with the usual morning chatter. Students hurried to their lockers, exchanged greetings, and discussed the latest gossip. Amidst this lively atmosphere, Aarushi's life seemed perfect. She had great friends, did well in her classes, and had just started dating the charming new student, Rahul. Little did she know, her seemingly perfect world was about to be turned upside down.

From the moment Rahul stepped into her life, there was an undeniable spark. Their connection felt effortless, and their budding romance quickly became the talk of the school. Aarushi couldn't believe her luck; Rahul was everything she had ever wanted.

But life has a way of throwing curveballs when we least expect them. Behind Rahul's dazzling smile and affectionate gestures lay a secret that would challenge everything Aarushi thought she knew about love and trust. It was a secret shared only with his closest friend, Sameer, whose presence was always shadowed by an air of mystery.

As the days turned into weeks, Aarushi noticed subtle changes in Rahul's behavior, but her trust in him remained unshaken. She was unaware that her journey would soon take her through a maze of emotions and revelations that would test her strength and resilience.

In a world where appearances often deceive and the heart holds secrets too deep to reveal, Aarushi would come to learn that love is not always straightforward. It is twisted, complicated, and at times, painfully beautiful.

This is the story of Aarushi, Rahul, and Sameer—a tale of love, discovery, and the courage to face the truth. As you turn these pages, prepare to embark on a journey that explores the depth of human emotions and the unexpected paths that love can take.

Acknowledgments

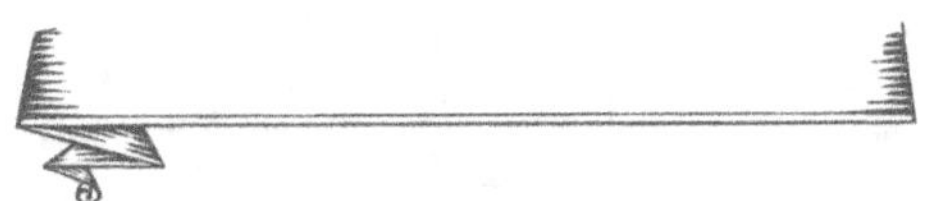

Writing Twisted Love has been an incredible journey filled with inspiration, learning, and growth. This book would not have been possible without the support, encouragement, and understanding of those who have been a part of my life throughout this process.

I extend my heartfelt gratitude to all the readers who have embraced this story. Your enthusiasm and engagement have been a source of motivation and joy.

To everyone who offered their insights, feedback, and constructive criticism—thank you. Your perspectives have helped shape this story into what it is today.

Lastly, to all those who believe in the power of love and its many forms, this book is for you. May it resonate with your experiences and inspire you to embrace the beautiful complexities of love.

Introduction

Love is a journey, often taking us on paths we least expect. It can be both uplifting and challenging, filled with moments of pure joy and deep introspection. Twisted Love delves into the intricate and multifaceted nature of love, portraying a story that is as complex as it is relatable.

Set against the backdrop of Greenwood High, this story follows Aarushi, a bright and ambitious student whose life takes an unexpected turn when she meets Rahul, the charming new student. Their instant connection blossoms into a romantic relationship, bringing happiness and excitement into Aarushi's life.

However, as their relationship deepens, Aarushi begins to notice subtle changes and unspoken truths that lead her to question everything she thought she knew about love and trust. Rahul's close friendship with Sameer, a quiet and mysterious figure, becomes a focal point of intrigue and confusion for Aarushi.

Through Aarushi's eyes, Twisted Love explores themes of self-discovery, acceptance, and the strength to navigate the unexpected twists of life. It highlights the importance of understanding and embracing the complexities of human relationships, and the resilience required to move forward in the face of challenges.

This book is an exploration of love in its many forms—romantic, platonic, and self-love. It is a reminder that while love can be complicated and sometimes painful, it is also a powerful force that shapes our lives and helps us grow.

As you immerse yourself in Aarushi's story, may you find reflections of your own experiences and the courage to embrace the twists and turns of your journey. Twisted Love is not just a story about relationships; it is a testament to the enduring spirit of love and the unexpected paths it leads us on.

Connect With Mrigendra,
Thank you very much for choosing this book.
You can also connect with me on Instagram,
https://www.instagram.com/i_mrigendrabharti.official
With Love,
Mrigendra Bharti

Chapter 1: New Beginnings

Part 1: The New Student

The bell rang, signaling the start of another day at Greenwood High. Aarushi hurried through the bustling corridors, waving to friends and exchanging quick greetings. She loved the energy of the school mornings, where everyone was full of anticipation for the day ahead.

Aarushi's best friend, Neha, caught up with her near the lockers. "Did you hear? There's a new student joining our class today," Neha said, her eyes sparkling with curiosity.

"Really? I wonder who it is," Aarushi replied, her interest piqued.

As they entered their classroom, the usual hum of chatter greeted them. The teacher, Mrs. Sharma, stood at the front, waiting for the students to settle down. Beside her was a boy Aarushi had never seen before. He had a confident stance, with dark hair that fell slightly over his eyes and a friendly smile that seemed to put everyone at ease.

"Class, this is Rahul," Mrs. Sharma announced. "He's new here, so I expect you all to make him feel welcome."

Aarushi watched as Rahul introduced himself and took a seat near the window. There was something about him that caught her attention, but she couldn't quite put her finger on it.

Throughout the morning, Aarushi found her thoughts drifting towards the new student. During lunch, she and Neha discussed their first impressions.

"He seems nice," Neha said, glancing over at Rahul, who was sitting a few tables away, already surrounded by a group of curious classmates.

"Yeah, he does," Aarushi agreed, still trying to figure out what it was about him that intrigued her.

Later that day, Aarushi was in the library, looking for a book for her history project, when she noticed Rahul standing in the same aisle. He was skimming through a book on ancient civilizations, seemingly engrossed.

"Hi," she said, walking up to him. "I'm Aarushi. Welcome to Greenwood High."

Rahul looked up and smiled. "Thanks, Aarushi. I'm still getting used to everything here, but everyone seems friendly."

"You'll get the hang of it soon," Aarushi replied. "If you need any help or have any questions, feel free to ask."

"Actually," Rahul said, "I could use some help finding my way around. This school is bigger than my last one."

"Sure, I can show you around," Aarushi offered. They spent the next few minutes talking about the school layout and their classes. Aarushi found herself enjoying the conversation; Rahul was easy to talk to and seemed genuinely interested in getting to know her.

As the final bell of the day rang, Rahul thanked Aarushi for her help. "I appreciate it, Aarushi. Maybe we can hang out sometime?"

"Yeah, I'd like that," Aarushi said, smiling as they walked out of the library together.

As Aarushi headed home that day, she felt a sense of excitement she hadn't felt in a while. Meeting Rahul had added a new spark to her routine, and she was curious to see where this new connection would lead.

Part 2: First Impressions

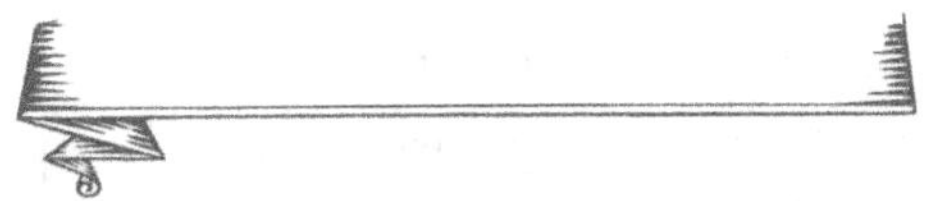

The next day at school, Aarushi couldn't help but look forward to seeing Rahul again. As she walked into the classroom, she noticed him already seated at his desk, engrossed in a conversation with Sameer, one of the quieter students in their class. She wondered how Rahul had managed to strike up a conversation with someone as reserved as Sameer so quickly.

During the first period, Aarushi tried to focus on the lesson, but her thoughts kept drifting back to Rahul. She found herself glancing in his direction more often than she intended. At one point, their eyes met, and he flashed her a quick, friendly smile. Aarushi felt her cheeks warm and quickly looked away, hoping no one had noticed.

At lunch, Aarushi and Neha grabbed their trays and headed to their usual spot. As they settled down, Rahul walked by, carrying his lunch tray. He hesitated for a moment before approaching them.

"Hey, mind if I join you guys?" he asked, looking between Aarushi and Neha.

"Of course, sit down," Aarushi said, feeling a flutter of excitement.

As Rahul took a seat, Neha started asking him questions about his previous school and his interests. Aarushi listened intently, occasionally chiming in. She learned that Rahul had moved from another city because of his father's job transfer. He liked playing basketball and had a keen interest in history, much like Aarushi herself.

"What about you, Aarushi? What do you like to do?" Rahul asked, turning his attention to her.

"Well, I love reading and painting," Aarushi replied. "And I'm on the school's debate team."

"That's cool," Rahul said, genuinely interested. "Maybe you can show me some of your paintings sometime."

Aarushi smiled. "Sure, I'd love to."

As the lunch period progressed, Aarushi noticed how effortlessly Rahul blended into their conversations. He had a natural charm and a way of making everyone around him feel comfortable. By the end of lunch, Neha was clearly impressed with Rahul, and Aarushi felt even more drawn to him.

Over the next few days, Aarushi and Rahul's interactions became more frequent. They found themselves partnering up for class projects and spending time together during breaks. Aarushi appreciated how easy it was to talk to Rahul; he listened intently and always had something interesting to say.

One afternoon, Aarushi and Rahul were sitting under a tree in the school courtyard, working on a history assignment. As they discussed their project, Aarushi found herself stealing glances at him, admiring his thoughtful expressions and the way his eyes lit up when he talked about something he was passionate about.

"You know," Rahul said, breaking her train of thought, "I'm really glad I met you, Aarushi. You've made my transition to this new school so much easier."

Aarushi felt her heart skip a beat. "I'm glad I met you too, Rahul. It's been great getting to know you."

As they packed up their things and headed back to class, Aarushi couldn't help but feel that her life was changing in unexpected and wonderful ways. She didn't know where this new friendship with Rahul would lead, but she was excited to find out.

Part 3: Building Friendship

As the weeks passed, Aarushi and Rahul's friendship continued to grow stronger. They found themselves spending more time together, both inside and outside of school. Their shared interests and easy conversation made it natural for them to become close friends.

One Saturday afternoon, Aarushi invited Rahul to her house to work on their history project. They set up their work in the living room, spreading out books and notes across the coffee table.

"Your house is really nice," Rahul said, looking around appreciatively.

"Thanks," Aarushi replied with a smile. "My mom loves decorating."

As they worked, Aarushi felt a growing sense of ease and comfort around Rahul. He had a way of making even the most mundane tasks enjoyable. They joked and laughed, sharing stories from their pasts and dreams for the future.

"Do you play any sports?" Rahul asked, taking a break from writing notes.

"I used to play badminton, but I haven't had much time lately," Aarushi admitted. "What about you?"

"I play basketball," Rahul said. "Maybe we can play a game sometime?"

"That sounds fun," Aarushi agreed. "I'd love to."

After they finished their work, Aarushi suggested they take a break in the garden. They stepped outside, enjoying the cool breeze and the scent of blooming flowers. Aarushi's dog, Max, bounded up to them, wagging his tail excitedly.

"He's adorable," Rahul said, kneeling down to pet Max.

"Thanks," Aarushi said, watching them with a smile. "He's my best buddy."

As the afternoon turned into evening, Rahul received a call from Sameer. Aarushi watched as his face lit up, and he stepped away to take the call. She noticed the ease and familiarity in Rahul's voice as he talked to Sameer, and she felt a pang of curiosity about their friendship.

When Rahul returned, Aarushi asked, "How do you know Sameer? You two seem pretty close."

"Sameer and I have been friends since we were kids," Rahul explained. "We used to live in the same neighborhood before I moved here. He's like a brother to me."

"That's nice," Aarushi said, feeling a bit more at ease. "It's good to have someone you're that close to."

Rahul nodded. "Yeah, he's been there for me through a lot."

The bond between Rahul and Sameer intrigued Aarushi, but she decided not to dwell on it too much. She was happy to see Rahul had someone he trusted so deeply.

As the evening came to a close, Rahul thanked Aarushi for the lovely time. "I had a great day, Aarushi. Thanks for inviting me over."

"Anytime," Aarushi replied warmly. "It was fun. Let's do it again soon."

As Rahul left, Aarushi felt a sense of contentment. She was grateful for their growing friendship and excited about the possibilities it held. Little did she know, the path ahead would be filled with unexpected twists that would challenge everything she thought she knew about love and friendship.

Part 4: The Spark

Aarushi couldn't shake off the feeling of warmth that lingered after Rahul's visit. His presence had brought a sense of joy and excitement into her life that she hadn't felt in a long time. She found herself eagerly looking forward to their next interaction, cherishing the growing bond between them.

One afternoon, as Aarushi was leaving school, she spotted Rahul waiting for her by the gate. His face broke into a smile when he saw her, and he waved her over.

"Hey, Aarushi! I was hoping we could hang out for a bit," Rahul said, falling into step beside her.

"Sure, I'd love to," Aarushi replied, feeling a flutter of excitement in her chest.

As they walked, Rahul shared stories from his old neighborhood, painting vivid pictures of his childhood adventures with Sameer. Aarushi listened intently, fascinated by the bond between Rahul and his childhood friend.

They eventually found themselves at a small café near the school. Aarushi ordered her favorite latte, while Rahul opted for a cappuccino. They settled into a cozy corner booth, enjoying the warm ambiance of the café.

As they talked, Aarushi couldn't help but notice how Rahul's eyes lit up when he spoke about his passions and dreams. He was so full of life and enthusiasm, and she found herself drawn to his magnetic personality.

Their conversation flowed effortlessly, touching on everything from their favorite books to their future aspirations. Aarushi felt a sense of connection with Rahul that she hadn't experienced with anyone else before. It was as if they were two pieces of a puzzle that had finally found their perfect fit.

As the evening wore on, Aarushi realized with a start that they had been talking for hours. She glanced at her phone and saw that it was already past sunset.

"I should probably head home," Aarushi said reluctantly, not wanting their time together to end.

"Yeah, me too," Rahul replied, a hint of disappointment in his voice.

As they walked back to school, Aarushi couldn't shake off the feeling that something special was brewing between them. She had never felt this comfortable and understood around someone before, and it both excited and scared her.

When they reached the school gate, Rahul turned to Aarushi with a smile. "Thanks for today, Aarushi. I had a great time."

"Me too," Aarushi said, returning his smile. "Let's do it again soon."

As Rahul walked away, Aarushi felt a sense of exhilaration coursing through her veins. She knew that this was just the beginning of something incredible, and she couldn't wait to see where their friendship would take them.

Chapter 2: Growing Closer

Part 1: Confession

Aarushi couldn't shake off the lingering warmth from her time with Rahul. His presence had become a constant in her thoughts, filling her days with excitement and anticipation. She found herself counting down the minutes until they could be together again, cherishing every moment they shared.

One afternoon, after school, Rahul asked if they could talk privately. Aarushi's heart raced with anticipation as they found a quiet spot in the school courtyard.

"Is everything okay?" Aarushi asked, concern evident in her voice.

Rahul took a deep breath, his gaze intense as he looked at her. "Aarushi, there's something I need to tell you."

Aarushi felt a knot form in her stomach, her mind racing with all sorts of possibilities. "What is it?" she asked, trying to keep her voice steady.

Rahul hesitated for a moment before speaking. "I... I really value our friendship, Aarushi. You mean a lot to me."

Aarushi felt a surge of relief wash over her. "You mean a lot to me too, Rahul," she said, smiling.

Rahul's expression softened, but there was a hint of something else in his eyes. "There's something else I need to tell you," he said, his voice barely above a whisper.

Aarushi's heart skipped a beat as she waited for him to continue. She could sense the gravity of his words, and her mind raced with possibilities.

"I... I think I'm starting to have feelings for you, Aarushi," Rahul confessed, his gaze searching hers for a reaction.

Aarushi felt her breath catch in her throat as she processed his words. She had never expected Rahul to feel this way about her, and yet, she couldn't deny the flutter of excitement that blossomed in her chest.

"I... I don't know what to say," Aarushi stammered, her mind reeling with a whirlwind of emotions.

Rahul reached out and took her hand in his, his touch sending shivers down her spine. "I understand if you don't feel the same way, Aarushi. I just needed to be honest with you."

Aarushi looked into Rahul's eyes, seeing the vulnerability and sincerity reflected in them. She realized in that moment that she felt the same way about him, that her feelings for him ran deeper than she had ever imagined.

"I... I think I feel the same way, Rahul," Aarushi confessed, her voice barely above a whisper.

A smile spread across Rahul's face, his eyes lighting up with joy. "Really?" he asked, his voice filled with hope.

Aarushi nodded, a wave of relief washing over her. "Really."

In that moment, everything else faded away as Rahul pulled her into a tight embrace. Aarushi felt like she was flying, her heart soaring with happiness as she realized that this was just the beginning of their journey together.

Part 2: Happy Moments

After Rahul's confession, a new dynamic blossomed between Aarushi and him. Their friendship evolved into something deeper, filled with moments of joy and happiness. They spent their days together, exploring new places, sharing laughter, and basking in the warmth of each other's company.

One sunny Saturday afternoon, Aarushi and Rahul decided to visit the local park. They strolled hand in hand along the winding paths, enjoying the gentle breeze and the vibrant colors of the blooming flowers. The world seemed to fade away as they lost themselves in each other's presence.

As they settled down on a bench overlooking the pond, Rahul reached into his bag and pulled out a sketchbook and a set of pencils. "I didn't tell you this, but I love to draw," he said, a sheepish smile playing on his lips.

Aarushi's eyes lit up with excitement. "Really? I'd love to see your drawings."

Rahul nodded, flipping open the sketchbook to reveal a collection of intricate sketches. Aarushi was amazed by the depth and detail in each drawing, feeling like she was peering into Rahul's soul with every stroke of his pencil.

"These are incredible, Rahul," Aarushi said, her admiration evident in her voice.

Rahul shrugged, a hint of embarrassment coloring his cheeks. "Thanks. It's just something I do to pass the time."

But Aarushi could see the passion and talent that Rahul possessed, and she encouraged him to pursue his artistic interests further. They spent the rest of the afternoon sketching together, lost in the world of their imaginations.

As the sun began to set, Aarushi and Rahul reluctantly packed up their things and started making their way home. The golden hues of the sunset painted the sky in breathtaking colors, casting a warm glow over everything around them.

As they walked, Aarushi couldn't help but feel a sense of contentment wash over her. Being with Rahul felt like coming home, like she had finally found where she belonged. She knew that their journey together was just beginning, and she was excited to see where it would lead.

As they reached Aarushi's house, Rahul turned to her with a smile. "Thanks for today, Aarushi. I had a great time."

"Me too," Aarushi replied, returning his smile. "Let's do it again soon."

As Rahul walked away, Aarushi watched him go, feeling a sense of happiness that she hadn't felt in a long time. She knew that Rahul had brought a new spark into her life, and she couldn't wait to see where their relationship would take them next.

Part 3: Introduction of Sameer

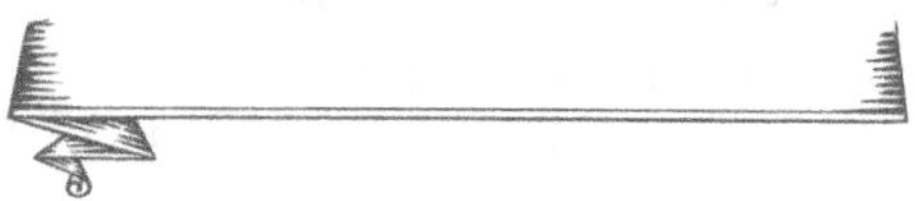

As Aarushi and Rahul's bond deepened, Aarushi couldn't help but notice Rahul's close relationship with Sameer. Sameer was a quiet and reserved boy, often seen in Rahul's company. While Aarushi had initially found their friendship endearing, she couldn't shake off a nagging curiosity about the depth of their connection.

One afternoon, during a study session at Rahul's house, Aarushi finally decided to broach the topic. As they pored over their textbooks, Aarushi couldn't contain her curiosity any longer.

"Rahul, can I ask you something?" Aarushi said, glancing up from her notes.

"Of course, what's on your mind?" Rahul replied, looking up with a warm smile.

"I've noticed how close you and Sameer are. How did you guys meet?" Aarushi asked, trying to sound casual.

A flicker of emotion passed over Rahul's face before he replied, "Sameer and I have been friends for as long as I can remember. We grew up together in the same neighborhood."

Aarushi nodded, intrigued by Rahul's response. "That's nice. You guys seem really close."

Rahul smiled, but there was a hint of sadness in his eyes. "Yeah, Sameer is like a brother to me. We've been through a lot together."

Aarushi sensed that there was more to the story than Rahul was letting on, but she didn't press further. She respected Rahul's privacy and didn't want to pry into his personal life.

As the evening wore on, Aarushi couldn't shake off the feeling of unease that lingered in the air. There was something about Rahul and Sameer's friendship that didn't sit right with her, but she couldn't quite put her finger on it.

As she left Rahul's house that evening, Aarushi couldn't shake off the nagging feeling of doubt that gnawed at her insides. She knew that she needed to trust Rahul and his judgment, but a part of her couldn't shake off the feeling that there was more to Rahul and Sameer's friendship than met the eye.

Little did Aarushi know, the truth about Rahul and Sameer's relationship would soon come to light, shattering her world and forcing her to confront the harsh realities of love and friendship.

Part 4: Unraveling Truths

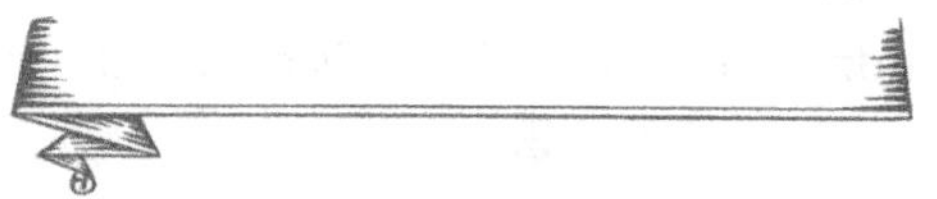

As days turned into weeks, Aarushi's unease about Rahul and Sameer's friendship continued to grow. She couldn't shake off the feeling that there was something Rahul wasn't telling her, something hidden beneath the surface of their seemingly perfect relationship.

One evening, while Aarushi was studying in her room, her phone buzzed with a message from Neha. It was a screenshot of a social media post, accompanied by a cryptic message: "Have you seen this?"

Aarushi's heart skipped a beat as she opened the message and read the caption beneath the photo. It was a picture of Rahul and Sameer, their arms wrapped around each other, with a caption that read, "Brothers for life."

Aarushi felt a cold shiver run down her spine as she stared at the photo. She couldn't believe what she was seeing. The intimacy between Rahul and Sameer in the photo sent alarm bells ringing in her mind, raising questions she didn't want to ask.

Her mind raced with possibilities, each more unsettling than the last. Had she been blind to the truth all along? Was there something more than friendship between Rahul and Sameer? And if so, what did that mean for her and Rahul's relationship?

Unable to shake off the feeling of dread that gripped her, Aarushi decided to confront Rahul about the photo. She dialed his number, her heart pounding in her chest as she waited for him to pick up.

"Hey, Aarushi, what's up?" Rahul's voice sounded cheerful on the other end of the line.

"Rahul, I need to talk to you about something," Aarushi said, trying to keep her voice steady.

"Of course, what's wrong?" Rahul replied, his tone shifting to concern.

Aarushi took a deep breath, steeling herself for what she was about to say. "I saw the photo of you and Sameer on social media. What's going on, Rahul? Why didn't you tell me about your relationship with him?"

There was a long pause on the other end of the line, and Aarushi's heart raced with anticipation. She held her breath, waiting for Rahul's response.

Finally, Rahul spoke, his voice heavy with emotion. "Aarushi, I'm sorry I didn't tell you sooner. Sameer is more than just a friend to me. He's my ex-boyfriend."

Aarushi felt like the ground had been pulled out from beneath her feet. She struggled to process Rahul's words, her mind reeling with shock and disbelief.

"I... I don't understand," Aarushi stammered, her voice trembling with emotion. "Why didn't you tell me?"

Rahul sighed, his voice filled with regret. "I was afraid of losing you, Aarushi. I didn't know how you would react if you found out about my past with Sameer. I'm sorry for keeping this from you."

As the truth of Rahul's confession sank in, Aarushi felt a tidal wave of emotions wash over her. She was hurt, angry, and confused, but beneath it all, she felt a glimmer of understanding. She realized that Rahul's love for her had never wavered, that he had been trying to protect their relationship from the harsh realities of his past.

In that moment, Aarushi knew that she had a choice to make. She could walk away from Rahul and his complicated past, or she could embrace the truth and stand by him through thick and thin.

Chapter 3: Facing Reality

Part 1: Aarushi's Decision

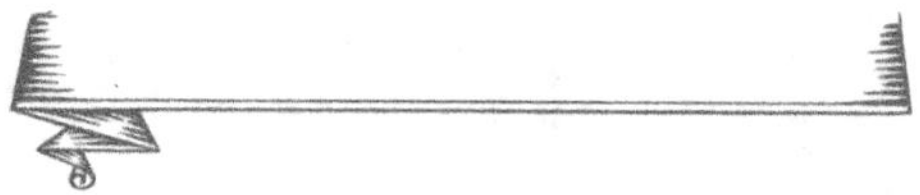

Aarushi's world felt like it had been turned upside down by Rahul's confession about his past with Sameer. She spent sleepless nights tossing and turning, trying to make sense of her emotions and the implications of Rahul's revelation. But amidst the chaos of her thoughts, one thing remained clear: she couldn't ignore her feelings for Rahul, no matter how complicated things had become.

One afternoon, Aarushi decided to meet Rahul at their usual spot in the school courtyard. She needed to talk to him, to confront the truth of his past and to make sense of where they stood now.

As Rahul approached, Aarushi could see the worry etched on his face. She took a deep breath, steeling herself for the conversation that was about to unfold.

"Rahul, we need to talk," Aarushi said, her voice steady despite the tumult of emotions swirling inside her.

Rahul nodded, his eyes filled with apprehension. "I know, Aarushi. I'm so sorry for keeping this from you."

Aarushi held up a hand, silencing him. "I need you to be honest with me, Rahul. I need to know everything about your relationship with Sameer."

Rahul took a deep breath, his gaze never leaving hers. "Sameer and I were in a relationship for a few years before I moved here. We were deeply in love, but things didn't work out between us. When I met you, I knew I had to leave my past behind and focus on building a future with you."

Aarushi listened intently, her heart aching at the pain she heard in Rahul's voice. She realized that despite the mistakes he had made, Rahul had always been honest with her about his feelings.

"I understand, Rahul," Aarushi said, reaching out to take his hand in hers. "I may not have expected this, but I'm willing to work through it with you. Our relationship may be complicated, but I believe in us."

Rahul's eyes filled with tears as he pulled Aarushi into a tight embrace. "Thank you, Aarushi. You have no idea how much this means to me."

As they held each other, Aarushi felt a sense of peace wash over her. She knew that their journey together wouldn't be easy, but she was willing to face whatever challenges came their way, as long as they faced them together.

Part 2: Navigating Challenges

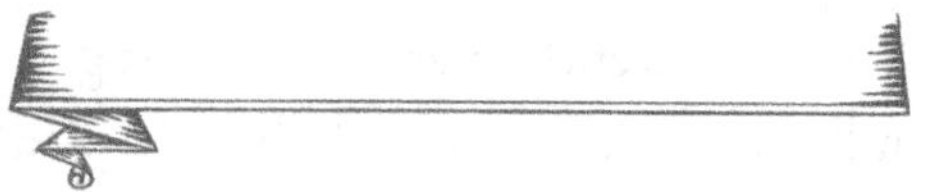

In the days that followed Aarushi and Rahul's heart-to-heart conversation, they found themselves navigating the complexities of their relationship with a newfound sense of determination and understanding. Despite the challenges they faced, they were committed to facing them together, united in their love for each other.

One afternoon, as they sat together in the school library, Aarushi noticed Rahul's distant expression. She reached out and gently touched his hand, drawing him out of his thoughts.

"Is everything okay, Rahul?" she asked, concern evident in her voice.

Rahul sighed, running a hand through his hair. "I've been thinking about Sameer a lot lately. I miss him, Aarushi, but I know I can't go back to the way things were."

Aarushi squeezed Rahul's hand reassuringly. "I understand, Rahul. It's okay to miss him, but remember that we're in this together. I'm here for you, no matter what."

Rahul nodded, a small smile tugging at the corners of his lips. "Thank you, Aarushi. I don't know what I'd do without you."

As they sat together in silence, Aarushi felt a sense of gratitude wash over her. Despite the challenges they faced, she knew that their love was stronger than any obstacle that stood in their way.

Later that week, Aarushi decided to invite Rahul over to her house for dinner. She wanted to spend quality time together away from the distractions of school and their social lives.

As they sat down to dinner, Aarushi's parents welcomed Rahul with open arms, making him feel like part of the family. Aarushi watched with a smile as Rahul laughed and joked with her parents, feeling a sense of warmth and belonging that she hadn't felt in a long time.

After dinner, Aarushi and Rahul retreated to her room to watch a movie. They cuddled up on the couch, lost in the world of the film as they laughed and cried together.

As the credits rolled, Aarushi looked over at Rahul, feeling a surge of love and gratitude for the man sitting beside her. She knew that their journey together wouldn't always be easy, but she was grateful for every moment they shared, knowing that they were stronger together than they could ever be apart.

Part 3: Unexpected Encounters

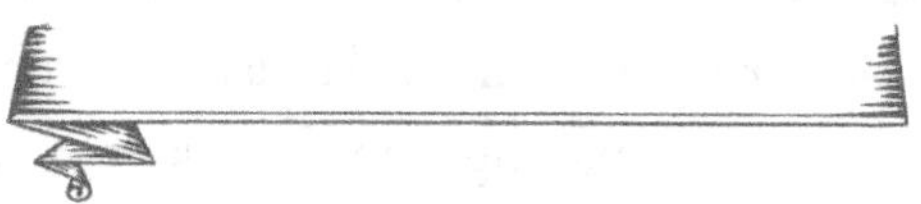

As Aarushi and Rahul continued to navigate the ups and downs of their relationship, they found themselves facing unexpected challenges that tested the strength of their bond.

One evening, as Aarushi was walking home from school, she spotted Sameer standing on the sidewalk, his eyes fixed on her with a mixture of sadness and longing. She felt a knot form in her stomach as she approached him, unsure of what to say.

"Sameer, what are you doing here?" Aarushi asked, her voice tinged with apprehension.

Sameer looked away, his shoulders slumped in defeat. "I needed to see you, Aarushi. I needed to talk to you."

Aarushi felt a surge of conflicting emotions wash over her. She couldn't deny the history and connection she shared with Sameer, but she also couldn't ignore the love she felt for Rahul.

"Sameer, I... I don't know what to say," Aarushi said, her voice trembling with uncertainty.

Sameer reached out and took her hand in his, his touch sending a jolt of electricity through her veins. "Aarushi, I know I messed up. I know I hurt you, and I'm sorry. But I still love you, Aarushi. I never stopped loving you."

Aarushi felt tears prick at the corners of her eyes as she looked into Sameer's pleading gaze. She knew that she had to be honest with him, even if it meant breaking his heart all over again.

"Sameer, I... I care about you, but I'm in love with Rahul," Aarushi confessed, her voice barely above a whisper.

Sameer's face fell, his eyes filled with pain. "I understand, Aarushi. I just needed to hear it from you."

As Sameer walked away, Aarushi felt a sense of sadness wash over her. She hated to see him in pain, but she knew that she had made the right choice in choosing Rahul.

Later that evening, Aarushi confided in Rahul about her encounter with Sameer. She expected him to be angry or jealous, but to her surprise, he was understanding and supportive.

"Aarushi, I trust you," Rahul said, wrapping his arms around her. "I know that you're committed to our relationship, and that's all that matters to me."

In that moment, Aarushi knew that she had found someone who loved her unconditionally, someone who would stand by her through thick and thin. And as she melted into Rahul's embrace, she felt a sense of peace wash over her, knowing that they were in this together, no matter what the future held.

Part 4: Trust and Loyalty

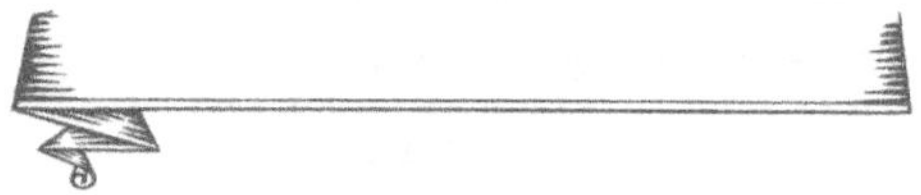

As Aarushi and Rahul navigated the complexities of their relationship, they found themselves leaning on each other more than ever before. With each passing day, their bond grew stronger, forged in the fires of adversity and tested by the trials of life.

One afternoon, as they sat together in the school courtyard, Aarushi noticed a group of girls whispering and casting furtive glances in their direction. She felt a pang of unease in the pit of her stomach, wondering what they were saying about her and Rahul.

"Rahul, have you noticed those girls staring at us?" Aarushi asked, her voice tinged with apprehension.

Rahul glanced over at the group, his expression unreadable. "Yeah, I've noticed. But let's not let them get to us, Aarushi. We know the truth about our relationship, and that's all that matters."

Aarushi nodded, feeling reassured by Rahul's words. She knew that they had faced far greater challenges than a few gossiping classmates, and she refused to let their negativity poison the love she shared with Rahul.

Later that week, Aarushi received a text message from Neha, asking if she wanted to hang out after school. Aarushi was hesitant at first, unsure of how Neha would react to her relationship with Rahul, but she ultimately decided to meet up with her friend.

As they sat together in a nearby café, Neha couldn't contain her curiosity any longer. "Aarushi, I've been meaning to ask you about Rahul. Are you two... you know, together?"

Aarushi hesitated for a moment, unsure of how to respond. But then she looked into Neha's eyes, seeing nothing but genuine concern and curiosity.

"Yes, Neha, Rahul and I are together," Aarushi admitted, a small smile playing on her lips.

Neha's eyes widened in surprise, but then she smiled, reaching out to squeeze Aarushi's hand. "I'm happy for you, Aarushi. You deserve to be with someone who makes you happy."

Aarushi felt a wave of gratitude wash over her as she realized just how lucky she was to have friends like Neha who supported her unconditionally. She knew that with their love and support, she and Rahul could overcome any obstacle that stood in their way.

As she left the café that evening, Aarushi felt a sense of peace settle over her. She knew that the road ahead wouldn't always be easy, but she was ready to face whatever challenges came their way, hand in hand with Rahul by her side.

Chapter 4: Turbulent Waters

Part 1: The Storm Approaches

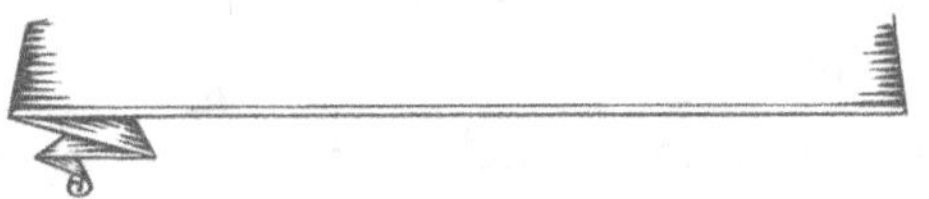

As Aarushi and Rahul's relationship continued to flourish, they found themselves sailing through calm waters, basking in the warmth of their love. But little did they know, a storm was brewing on the horizon, threatening to test the strength of their bond like never before.

One evening, as Aarushi was scrolling through her social media feed, she stumbled upon a photo that stopped her in her tracks. It was a picture of Rahul and Sameer, their arms wrapped around each other, with a caption that sent a chill down Aarushi's spine.

"Reunited with my love. ♥ #foreverandalways"

Aarushi's heart pounded in her chest as she stared at the photo, her mind racing with a whirlwind of emotions. She couldn't believe what she was seeing. How could Rahul be with Sameer when he had promised to leave his past behind?

With trembling hands, Aarushi dialed Rahul's number, her heart pounding in her chest as she waited for him to pick up.

"Hey, Aarushi, what's up?" Rahul's voice sounded cheerful on the other end of the line.

"Rahul, what is this?" Aarushi demanded, her voice trembling with anger and hurt.

There was a long pause on the other end of the line, and when Rahul finally spoke, his voice was filled with guilt and regret. "Aarushi, I can explain..."

But Aarushi didn't want to hear his excuses. She felt like her world was crumbling around her, and she couldn't bear to listen to Rahul's lies any longer.

"I trusted you, Rahul. I believed in us, but you've betrayed me," Aarushi said, her voice breaking with emotion. "I can't do this anymore. We're done."

With that, Aarushi hung up the phone, her hands shaking with rage and hurt. She couldn't believe that Rahul had lied to her, that he had broken her trust so completely.

As tears streamed down her face, Aarushi felt a sense of emptiness wash over her. She had never felt so alone, so betrayed, and she didn't know how she would ever be able to pick up the pieces of her shattered heart.

But little did she know, the storm that had torn her world apart was just the beginning of a journey that would test her in ways she never thought possible. And as she braced herself for the trials ahead, she knew that she would emerge from the darkness stronger and wiser than she had ever been before.

Part 2: Confrontation

In the aftermath of Aarushi's confrontation with Rahul, her mind was a whirlwind of conflicting emotions. She couldn't shake off the feeling of betrayal that gnawed at her heart, but amidst the pain, a steely resolve began to take root.

Determined to seek closure, Aarushi decided to confront Rahul in person. She needed answers, and she refused to let him off the hook without facing the consequences of his actions.

As she marched towards Rahul's house, her footsteps echoing in the silence of the night, Aarushi felt a sense of determination coursing through her veins. She had trusted Rahul with her heart, and he had shattered that trust without a second thought. But now, it was time for him to face the consequences of his betrayal.

When she reached Rahul's doorstep, Aarushi took a deep breath to steady her nerves before ringing the doorbell. Moments later, Rahul appeared, his expression a mix of surprise and guilt when he saw her standing there.

"Aarushi, what are you doing here?" Rahul asked, his voice tinged with apprehension.

Aarushi didn't mince words. "We need to talk, Rahul. Now."

Without waiting for a response, she pushed past him and stormed into the house, her heart pounding in her chest with each step she took. She couldn't afford to let her emotions get the best of her. She needed to stay strong, to confront Rahul with the full force of her anger and hurt.

When they reached Rahul's room, Aarushi turned to face him, her eyes blazing with intensity. "How could you do this to me, Rahul? How could you betray my trust like that?"

Rahul hung his head, unable to meet her gaze. "I'm sorry, Aarushi. I never meant to hurt you. I just... I didn't know how to tell you about Sameer."

Aarushi felt a surge of anger rise within her. "That's not good enough, Rahul. You lied to me, over and over again. You made me believe that you were committed to our relationship, but all along, you were still involved with Sameer."

Rahul reached out to take her hand, but Aarushi pulled away, her eyes flashing with anger. "Don't touch me, Rahul. I trusted you, and you betrayed that trust. I don't know if I can ever forgive you for that."

As the weight of her words hung heavy in the air, Aarushi felt a sense of catharsis wash over her. She had finally confronted Rahul about his betrayal, and now, it was up to him to prove whether he was worthy of her forgiveness.

Part 3: Reflections in the Storm

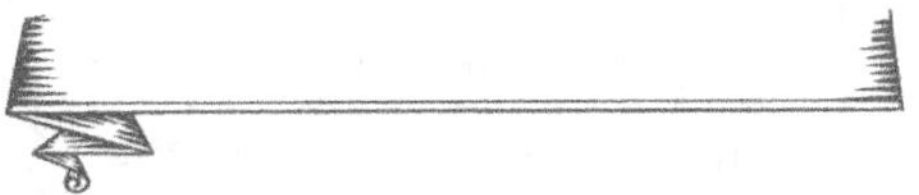

As Aarushi stormed out of Rahul's house, her heart heavy with pain and betrayal, she found herself grappling with a whirlwind of emotions. The night air felt cold against her skin as she wandered aimlessly through the streets, her mind consumed by thoughts of what could have been.

With each step she took, memories of her time with Rahul flooded her mind: the laughter they shared, the dreams they had woven together, the promises of a future filled with love and happiness. But now, all of that felt like nothing more than a distant dream, shattered by the harsh reality of Rahul's betrayal.

As she reached a nearby park, Aarushi sank onto a bench, her head in her hands as tears streamed down her face. She had given her heart to Rahul, only to have it broken into a million pieces. She couldn't shake off the feeling of emptiness that gnawed at her soul, leaving her feeling adrift in a sea of uncertainty.

But amidst the pain, a flicker of determination began to take root within Aarushi's heart. She refused to let Rahul's betrayal define her, to let it overshadow the love and strength that lay within her. She knew that she deserved better than someone who couldn't be honest with her, who couldn't honor the commitment they had made to each other.

With a newfound resolve, Aarushi wiped away her tears and straightened her shoulders, ready to face whatever lay ahead. She didn't know what the future held, but she knew that she would emerge from this storm stronger and more resilient than ever before.

As she made her way home, Aarushi couldn't shake off the feeling of uncertainty that lingered in the air. She knew that her journey was far from over, that there were still challenges and obstacles ahead of her. But she also knew that she had the strength and courage to face whatever came her way, to rise above the storm and find her own path to happiness.

And as she stepped into the warmth and safety of her home, surrounded by the love and support of her family, Aarushi felt a glimmer of hope ignite within her heart. She knew that no matter what the future held, she would never be alone, for she had the love of those who mattered most to guide her through the darkness and into the light.

Part 4: Finding Strength

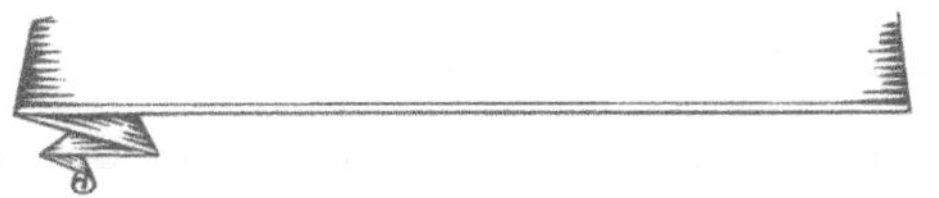

In the days that followed her confrontation with Rahul, Aarushi found herself grappling with a tumultuous mix of emotions. While the pain of betrayal still lingered, she refused to let it consume her. Instead, she focused on finding the strength within herself to move forward and rebuild her life.

With the unwavering support of her family and friends, Aarushi began to pick up the pieces of her shattered heart. She threw herself into her studies and extracurricular activities, finding solace in the familiar rhythms of school and the camaraderie of her peers.

But amidst the busyness of her daily life, Aarushi couldn't shake off the feeling of emptiness that lingered within her. She missed Rahul, despite the hurt he had caused her, and she couldn't help but wonder what could have been if things had turned out differently between them.

One afternoon, as she sat alone in her room, lost in thought, Aarushi's phone buzzed with a message from Neha. It was a simple invitation to hang out, but to Aarushi, it felt like a lifeline in the midst of her turmoil.

Gathering her courage, Aarushi accepted Neha's invitation and met up with her friend at a nearby café. As they sat together, sipping on their drinks and chatting about everything and nothing, Aarushi felt a sense of peace wash over her.

Neha listened patiently as Aarushi poured out her heart, offering words of comfort and encouragement. She reminded Aarushi of her worth, of the strength and resilience that lay within her, waiting to be unleashed.

"You're going to get through this, Aarushi," Neha said, her voice filled with conviction. "You're stronger than you know, and you have so much love and support surrounding you. Don't ever forget that."

As Aarushi listened to Neha's words, a spark of hope ignited within her heart. She realized that she didn't need someone else to define her happiness, that she had the power to create her own destiny and forge her own path to fulfillment.

With Neha by her side, Aarushi knew that she could weather any storm that came her way. She was ready to embrace the challenges and uncertainties of the future, knowing that she had the strength and resilience to overcome whatever obstacles stood in her way.

As she bid Neha goodbye and made her way home, Aarushi felt a sense of peace settle over her. She didn't know what the future held, but she knew that she was ready to face it head-on, armed with the love and support of those who mattered most.

Chapter 5: New Horizons

Part 1: A Fresh Start

With each passing day, Aarushi found herself growing stronger and more resilient in the face of adversity. She had come a long way since her confrontation with Rahul, and now, as she stood on the brink of a new chapter in her life, she felt a sense of excitement tinged with apprehension.

The start of a new school year brought with it a fresh opportunity for Aarushi to reinvent herself and carve out a path that was uniquely her own. With her head held high and her heart open to new possibilities, she stepped through the doors of the school, ready to embrace whatever challenges and adventures lay ahead.

As she made her way to her first class, Aarushi couldn't help but feel a sense of anticipation bubbling within her. She didn't know what the future held, but she was determined to make the most of every opportunity that came her way.

In the weeks that followed, Aarushi threw herself into her studies and extracurricular activities with renewed vigor. She sought out new friendships and forged connections with classmates who shared her passions and interests, finding comfort and camaraderie in their shared experiences.

But amidst the hustle and bustle of her busy life, Aarushi couldn't shake off the feeling of longing that lingered within her.

She missed the warmth and companionship she had shared with Rahul, despite the pain he had caused her, and she couldn't help but wonder if she would ever find love again.

One afternoon, as she sat alone in the school courtyard, lost in thought, Aarushi's reverie was interrupted by the sound of laughter and chatter nearby. Curious, she looked up to see a group of students gathered around a familiar face: Sameer.

Aarushi's heart skipped a beat as she watched Sameer interact with his classmates, his easy smile and infectious energy drawing people towards him like a magnet. Despite the pain of their past, Aarushi couldn't help but feel a twinge of curiosity about the boy she had once loved.

With a sense of determination coursing through her veins, Aarushi made her way over to where Sameer was standing, her heart pounding in her chest with each step she took. She didn't know what she would say to him, or if he would even want to talk to her, but she knew that she couldn't let fear hold her back from seizing the opportunity for closure.

As she approached Sameer, he looked up and met her gaze, his eyes widening in surprise at the sight of her. For a moment, they stood there in silence, the weight of their shared history hanging heavy in the air between them.

Then, with a tentative smile, Aarushi spoke. "Hi, Sameer. It's been a while."

Part 2: Reconnecting

As Aarushi stood before Sameer, her heart pounding in her chest, she couldn't help but feel a rush of emotions flood through her. It had been so long since they had last spoken, since their paths had diverged in ways neither of them could have predicted.

Sameer's expression softened as he took in Aarushi's presence, a hint of nostalgia flickering in his eyes. "Aarushi, it's good to see you," he said, his voice tinged with warmth.

Aarushi returned his smile, feeling a sense of relief wash over her. "It's good to see you too, Sameer. How have you been?"

They fell into an easy rhythm of conversation, catching up on the events of the past year and sharing stories about their lives since they had last seen each other. Despite the awkwardness that lingered beneath the surface of their interaction, Aarushi found herself feeling more at ease in Sameer's presence than she had expected.

As they talked, Aarushi couldn't help but marvel at how much had changed since they had last been together. Sameer had grown into a confident and charismatic young man, his passion for life shining through in everything he did. And though Aarushi knew that their relationship could never be what it once was, she couldn't deny the connection that still existed between them.

Before they knew it, the bell signaling the end of the lunch period rang out, jolting them back to reality. With a sense of reluctance, Aarushi and Sameer said their goodbyes, each lost in their own thoughts as they went their separate ways.

As Aarushi made her way to her next class, she couldn't shake off the feeling of nostalgia that lingered within her. Seeing Sameer again had stirred up memories and emotions that she had long buried, forcing her to confront the past in ways she hadn't expected.

But amidst the turmoil of her thoughts, Aarushi felt a sense of clarity begin to emerge. She realized that while her history with Sameer would always be a part of her, it didn't define who she was or dictate her future. She had grown and changed in ways she never thought possible, and she was ready to embrace the new horizons that lay ahead.

With a renewed sense of purpose, Aarushi stepped into her next class, her heart filled with hope and possibility. She didn't know what the future held, but she knew that she was ready to face it head-on, armed with the lessons she had learned and the strength she had gained along the way.

Part 3: Inner Turmoil

In the days that followed her unexpected encounter with Sameer, Aarushi found herself grappling with a whirlwind of emotions. Seeing him again had stirred up memories and feelings that she thought she had buried deep within her heart, and now, she couldn't shake off the sense of turmoil that lingered within her.

As she sat alone in her room, lost in thought, Aarushi couldn't help but replay their conversation over and over again in her mind. She found herself questioning the choices she had made and wondering what could have been if things had turned out differently between them.

Despite the pain of their past, Aarushi couldn't deny the lingering connection she felt with Sameer. There was something about him that drew her in, something magnetic and irresistible that she couldn't quite put into words.

But amidst the confusion and uncertainty, Aarushi knew that she couldn't afford to dwell on the past. She had worked so hard to rebuild her life and find happiness within herself, and she wasn't about to let Sameer's reappearance derail her progress.

With a sense of determination coursing through her veins, Aarushi made a conscious effort to focus on the present moment and the opportunities that lay ahead. She threw herself into her studies and extracurricular activities with renewed vigor, finding solace in the familiarity of her routines and the support of her friends.

But no matter how hard she tried to push him out of her mind, Sameer's presence lingered like a shadow, a constant reminder of the choices she had made and the paths she had chosen to follow.

One evening, as she sat alone in the school library, poring over her textbooks, Aarushi's phone buzzed with a text message. It was from Sameer, asking if she wanted to meet up and talk.

Aarushi's heart skipped a beat at the sight of his name on her screen, a mixture of apprehension and curiosity swirling within her. She knew that meeting up with Sameer would only complicate things further, but a part of her couldn't resist the pull of the past.

With a sense of trepidation, Aarushi typed out a response and hit send, agreeing to meet Sameer later that evening. As she closed her textbook and gathered her things, her mind raced with a thousand questions and uncertainties, but amidst the chaos, a small voice whispered within her heart, urging her to embrace the unknown and see where the path would lead.

Part 4: Facing the Past

As the time for her meeting with Sameer approached, Aarushi found herself filled with a mixture of nerves and anticipation. She couldn't shake off the feeling of uncertainty that gnawed at her, but a part of her also felt a glimmer of hope that perhaps this meeting would provide the closure she so desperately sought.

With a deep breath to steady her nerves, Aarushi made her way to the agreed-upon meeting spot, her heart pounding in her chest with each step she took. She didn't know what to expect, but she was determined to face whatever lay ahead with courage and resilience.

When she arrived, she found Sameer waiting for her, his expression a mix of apprehension and longing. For a moment, they stood there in silence, the weight of their shared history hanging heavy in the air between them.

Then, with a tentative smile, Sameer spoke. "Aarushi, thank you for meeting me. I know things between us ended badly, and I've regretted it every day since."

Aarushi felt a surge of emotions flood through her at Sameer's words. Despite the pain of their past, she couldn't deny the sincerity in his voice, the raw vulnerability that shone in his eyes.

"I've regretted it too, Sameer," Aarushi admitted, her voice barely above a whisper. "But we can't change the past. All we can do is learn from it and move forward."

Sameer nodded, his expression filled with understanding. "You're right, Aarushi. I know I hurt you, and I'm so sorry for that. I just hope that maybe, someday, we can find a way to move past it and start over."

Aarushi felt a flicker of hope ignite within her heart at Sameer's words. Despite the pain and heartache they had endured, she couldn't deny the connection that still existed between them, the lingering spark of something that had once been so beautiful and pure.

With a sense of resolve, Aarushi reached out and took Sameer's hand in hers, a silent gesture of forgiveness and reconciliation. "Maybe someday, Sameer. But for now, let's focus on the present and the possibilities that lie ahead."

As they stood there, hand in hand, Aarushi felt a sense of peace wash over her. She didn't know what the future held, but she knew that as long as she had the strength and courage to face it head-on, she could overcome any obstacle that stood in her way.

With Sameer by her side, Aarushi felt ready to embrace the new horizons that lay ahead, knowing that whatever challenges and adventures awaited her, she would face them with an open heart and a steadfast spirit.

Conclusion: Twisted Love

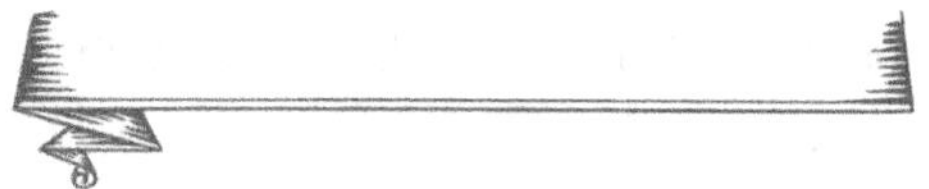

In the weeks that followed her meeting with Sameer, Aarushi found herself reflecting on the twists and turns that had brought her to this moment. She had come a long way since the pain and heartache of her past, and now, as she stood on the threshold of a new chapter in her life, she felt a sense of peace and clarity wash over her.

With Sameer by her side as a supportive friend, Aarushi had found the closure she had been seeking. She had come to terms with the mistakes of her past and had forgiven those who had hurt her, including herself. She realized that while she couldn't change the past, she could learn from it and use those lessons to shape a brighter future.

As she looked ahead, Aarushi felt a sense of excitement and anticipation bubbling within her. She had rediscovered her passion for life and was eager to embrace the opportunities and adventures that lay ahead. Whether it was pursuing her dreams, forging new friendships, or exploring new interests, she was ready to seize the day with courage and resilience.

But amidst the excitement of the future, Aarushi knew that she would always carry the memories of her past with her. They were a part of who she was, a testament to the strength and resilience that had carried her through the darkest moments of her life. And while she couldn't change the past, she could use it as a source of inspiration to create a future filled with love, laughter, and endless possibilities.

As she stepped into the warmth and sunshine of a new day, Aarushi felt a sense of gratitude wash over her. She was grateful for the lessons she had learned, the friendships she had forged, and the love that had sustained her through it all. And as she walked forward with her head held high and her heart open to new adventures, she knew that whatever the future held, she would face it with courage, grace, and an unwavering belief in the power of love to conquer all.

About the Author

Mrigendra Bharti, born on June 29, 2004, in South Delhi, India, is a multifaceted individual recognized as the owner of Mrigendra Bharti Group InfoTech India Co. Pvt Ltd. Beyond his entrepreneurial endeavors, he is a distinguished music producer, director, and a budding writer.

Embarking on his professional journey at a young age, Mrigendra Bharti's visionary leadership has led to the establishment of several successful ventures, including Croma Music Series Entertainment, Sellbrochure, Fauget Innovative, and more.

What sets Mrigendra apart is his early initiation into the world of business. His foray into the unknown realms of entrepreneurship began during his 10th-grade years, where he delved into the music industry. This initial venture laid the foundation for subsequent achievements, showcasing his dedication and resilience.

Having honed his skills in music, Mrigendra Bharti not only demonstrated significant growth in his craft but also expanded his professional network. His passion extends beyond music, encompassing app and website development, as well as graphic design.

Fueled by his creative aspirations, Mrigendra established the Mrigendra Bharti Group, a company specializing in website and app development. Currently, he collaborates with a dedicated team, collectively working on ambitious projects that promise innovation and excellence.

Mrigendra's journey serves as an inspiration, particularly for today's students, highlighting the potential of youthful determination and the ability to transform innovative ideas into successful businesses. As he continues to make strides in various domains, Mrigendra Bharti remains a dynamic force, contributing vibrancy to the realms of business, music, and technology.

Read more at https://www.imwriter-mrigendra.rf.gd.